A Ballet Dream

Short Story

By Nicole Marie Woodcock

Nicole Marie McKinney

Middletwon, Delware

© 2023 by Nicole Marie Woodcock. All rights reserved. No part of this publication may be reproduced, distributed, or transmitted, in any form or by any means, including photocopying, recording, or other electronic or mechanical methods, without the prior written permission of the author, expect in the case of brief quotations embodied in critical reviews and certain other noncommercial uses permitted by copyright laws. For permission requests, write to starofdreamsnmysteries@gmail.com

ISBN: 978-1-7369853-7-3

Library of Congress Control Number: 2023915954

Any references to historical events, real people, or places are fictitious. Names, characters, and places are products of the author's imagination.

Laura Luikart creates the cover from Sandy Signs Works, Meadville, Pennsylvania.

Printed in the United States of America.

This Book is dedicated to Carol Drury.

For her encouragement and friendship. And for her love of storytelling.

Serenity Amira Swanson stood across the street, looking at the San Francisco Ballet Company. She arrived an hour early, and butterflies fluttered low in her gut. Doubts started to trickle in her mind, for Serenity didn't have the training like other dancers; she was self-taught. But it was her time to prove she could better herself.

Taking another deep breath to center herself, she picked up her duffle bag and walked across the street with brisk strides straight into the building. She took notice of every detail with soulful brown eyes before moving toward a woman sitting at a table.

The woman shuffled through a stack of papers and gazed up, lips pinching. "My name is Julia, and I'll be signing you in today. Name?"

A hint of a smile pulled at Serenity's lips. "My name is Serenity Amira Swanson. I'm here for the audition." Julia glanced at the paperwork, made a checkmark, and handed Serenity a sticker with 329 stamped in bold numbers.

As Serenity placed the sticker on her chest, Julia pointed. "The studio is down the hall, the last door on the right."

"Thank you." Serenity strolled away. Stepping into the room, Serenity tilted her head back, basking in the rays pouring through the bay windows.

    Dropping her bag by a chair, she hastened to one of the mirrors on the wall and released her hair clip. Her pale blonde hair fell into waves, reaching her waist. She fingered through the strands and twisted them into a dancer's bun.

    Serenity opened her bag with shaking hands, removed her leg warmers, and switched shoes. She slipped off her sweater and placed them on top of the pile. She looked around the room, taking it all in, and sighed before heading to the barre and beginning her warm-ups, swinging her leg and rolling her shoulders. Toe touches, splits, and leg stretches followed.

Other dancers arrived with chatter and laughter that slowly died away. As they began stationing themselves, but Serenity was lost in her world with no sense of time. With each move, her body grew warm, her skin glistening. She went through the motions, and happiness spurted within her like a seed taking hold. Serenity was ready, body limber. Clapping pulled her attention toward the doorway where two women waited. Serenity jerked to attention, mouth dry, muscles twitching.

"Welcome to the San Francisco Ballet Company. I am Helgi, and this is Kelly. For the next several hours, we will put you through a series of different performances, and after each session, some of you will be eliminated."

Helgi eased back as Kelly stepped forward. "Welcome to the most intense moment of your life." Kelly held her hand out to a couple standing near the far wall. "Accompanying us is David and Jessica. They will lead you through a series of dance movements." She bowed her head as she eased back. "You may begin."

The hours drifted by, and only twice did Serenity have to ask for clarification on certain moves. A sense of relief came with each cut, filling Serenity with more confidence.

An emotional war broke out within Serenity. One moment her motions were elegant, but when Helgi and Kelly made their notes, watching her intently, it chilled her to the bone, but she forced herself to remain calm.

Training her gaze to a spot on the wall, Serenity twirled; it helped with the dizziness. She didn't need to trip or run into the person beside her. The cramping in her toes sent fire racing along her nerve endings, but she didn't dare relax.

Grinding her teeth, she forced herself through the pain.

The dancers slowly dwindled until only a few remained.

Serenity stood off to the side, wiping her head with a towel. Sweat trickled down her chest, back, and legs, making her form-fitting clothes stick tighter to her body. The others had spares; they had changed occasionally during the small breaks. She didn't have any extra, so she had to make due. Serenity sipped some water and inhaled deeply to bring her breathing under control.

"I need your attention, please." Kelly motioned to David and Jessica, and they brought chairs forward. The dancers sat. "Congratulations to the six of you for making it this far. This last dance will be judged for your talent alone. No instructions will be given. Stand along the wall, and you will be allotted two minutes to perform."

Kelly waved a person on from the back. "Mitchell, if you would please."

A tall man edged through the dancers, sat at the piano, and placed his fingers on the keys. The first dancer struck a pose as Mitchell pressed down on the ivory.

Serenity closed her eyes, soaking in the music and hoping she could pull through this, for it was a significant milestone. This audition would make or break her, and Serenity was undoubtedly hoping for the former.

I have to let it all go. The worries, pain, and sorrow. Right here and now. Give them up to the Lord and walk away, for they don't matter now. What matters is this moment. I will do this and execute the one jump I could never accomplish. I will have faith and push doubt behind me. Be with me, though, Lord.

Serenity watched each dance. William would get in for dominating the area out of all the performers. His relaxed nature radiated happiness. The three women and the two men towered over her, and their bodies held more muscle.

Serenity mentally scolded herself, thinking of what she needed to do, and a tiny smile broke free. A male's voice reached her ears. "Number 329, you're up."

She nodded at David.

Serenity closed her eyes, took two deep breaths, and steadied her heart with one last prayer.

With the first musical note, Serenity moved as if on stage. She ignored the judging eyes. Transitioning through a series of pirouettes, twirls, and leaps,

Serenity became lost in the music, resembling a leaf dancing in the wind.

    Her grace brought tears to the eyes of all in the room and kept them spellbound with the beauty of her movements as if she was bewitching them.

Saying a quick prayer, Serenity bound into a grand jete, a problematic jump for her. She flew through the air. One leg stretched out in front and the other behind, landing without a wobble. On the tips of her toes, she finished the last few steps before dropping into a seated position, hands resting at her sides as the music faded.

Silence filled the room. Serenity's heart pounded loudly in her ears, and her body trembled. She cast her eyes down, wanting to curl into herself and disappear. The first clapping hands, followed by the others, forced her gaze up.

Wonder adorned her face as

tears trickled down her cheeks,

and a smile broke free through

trembling lips.

To Serenity's ears, the

applause boomed as though

thunder echoed through the

room, and the cheers rained

down, adding to the storm. She eased her body off the floor, held her head high, and bowed, arms gracefully pushed out. "Thank you for your time."

William stepped close. "You were amazing."

"Thank you. You're not too bad yourself." Serenity bit her

lip and closed her eyes, cheeks warming.

"Attention, please." Helgi clapped. "There is a tie between numbers 345 and 440. And a tie between numbers 329 and 215." Moving her gaze over those not chosen, Helgi said, "For those whose time here has come to an end, we thank you and wish you luck with your future endeavors."

While the others withdrew from the room, Serenity frowned, knowing she could end up like those dancers next.

Julia stepped into the room. "Will you all follow me, please."

The dancers followed Julia back down the corridors to the sign-in table. "Have a seat. You may return to the studio for a private interview when I call you. After, you will come back here."

Another hour ticked by, and Serenity refused to eat,

despite the others opening snacks they brought. She perched on a chair in the hallway, back rigid, hands folded neatly in her lap, feet planted evenly on the ground, and her eyes trained ahead. Each contestant left yet returned shortly after.

"Swanson."

Serenity jumped, hand on her heart, and rose fluidly. She walked down the hall behind Julia. Serenity went to enter the room but felt Julia's hand on her wrist.

"Be honest and strong. Good luck."

She tilted her head at those five simple words, and the walls Serenity had built over the years crashed down. Nodding, she took a choppy breath and sighed. She walked into the room and stood before the four judges. Straightening her posture, Serenity turned her feet, taking a dancer's stance.

"You're unusual, Miss Swanson, due to your lack of training and experience. Tell us what you could offer us."

Serenity swallowed the lump in her throat. "I come from poverty where I have been neglected, ladies and gentlemen." Her voice cracked. "I have no money or even a place to call home. I'm self-taught, yet I'm willing to work hard and push myself to be the best I can be." Serenity lowered her eyes, willing the tears away, and released a shaking breath before meeting their gazes again. "All I can say is I will give you my all. I have nothing else to give but my heart and love for dancing."

A long pause seemed to follow, "Thank you for your time, Miss Swanson. Go back with the others, and we'll call you all back for the vote."

Serenity paused at the door and glanced back. "No, you shouldn't be thanking me. I should be thanking you."

Holding her head high, she proceeded down the hall back to the others. She felt a presence beside her. Looking over, she noticed William.

"They would be fools not to choose you."

Serenity gave him a questioning look. "Really?"

"Why wouldn't they? The pure adoration that appears on your face while dancing is reason enough. You're breathtaking, even angelic."

"I wish it was as easy as that."

Serenity bit her lip.

"It is, Serenity."

Serenity shook her head. "Believe it or not, I'm self-taught. I had to beg them even to consider me for the tryout."

"You made it this far with no professional training, young

lady. Many who didn't cut are professionals. That's saying something right there."

"But—"

"Please, follow me." Julia waved her hand towards the hall and started down.

They stood as a group and followed, but Alice yanked

Serenity back, a jealous look in her eyes. "Why are you even here? No one wants you."

Serenity looked down at Alice's hand, clenching her wrist. "You may be right. Nobody will want me. I've learned to live independently and have the same rights as you."

Pulling away, Serenity caught up to William.

"What was that about?" William's brow shot up.

She glanced over her shoulder toward Alice and

back to William. "Only someone being childish."

They eased back into the room and formed a straight line. Julia whispered something to the directors before leaving the room. As the judges jotted a few notes down, Helgi peered up. "Never before have we put any auditions to a vote, but we had to this time. We will ask each of you to perform one movement and one movement only, away from the mirrors, so you can't see yourselves or the others. Understood?"

"Yes," they agreed simultaneously.

"The position you will strike is Attitude." Helgi tapped a cane on the floor. "Begin."

Serenity thought through the steps as she rose on her toes and lifted her leg behind her body, bending her knee at an angle with her arms forming a hoop above her head. Muscles burning, she held the position.

She focused straight ahead, face impassive and teeth grinding behind firm lips.

With another rap of the cane, Helgi nodded.

Each eased from their poses, falling into their starting positions. They stood, waiting with bated breath, as the four judges whispered back and forth.

Kelly left her chair. "We have come to a decision. Usually, we send out letters, but we'll do this officially today." Kelly looked them each in the eye. "Mr. James Holland, your technique and performance were good, but you don't possess the nature we seek."

James bowed and shook hands with William. "Awesome job, man."

"Thank you. You gave me a challenge." Replied William as James grabbed his bag and left.

"We'd like to congratulate Mr. William Collions. The lead male position is yours."

Kelly turned her gaze to Serenity and Alice with an unreadable expression. She studied them for a time, yet something gave her pause when she went to speak. Kelly turned to her colleagues, whispering as they leaned in. Nodding, she straightened and faced the dancers. "Miss Alice Knapp, you are a fantastic dancer; however, your arch needs work. We will be in touch with you at a later time. "

Alice huffed, stomped to her bag, and left without a backward glance.

"We come to you, Miss Swanson. You will be the youngest dancer with no experience. Yet your talent is unmatched. Welcome aboard."

Serenity stumbled back, hand on her chest, and before she knew it, William swung her around, whispering in her ear, "I told you so."

As he lowered her to her feet, she turned toward the panel. "Thank you all so very much."

"Miss Swanson, we want our company therapist and doctor to assess you for nutrition and a health check. In the meantime, housing will need to be figured out."

"You don't have to."

"We take care of our own." Hegli smiled.

"Thank you." A blush appeared on Serenity's face.

"Hegli and Kelly, I have a spare room for her to use until the housing is taken care of." William squeezed Serenity's hand.

"Very good, William," Kelly said and returned to the table.

The judges gathered papers, and Helgi turned to the two, tilting her head to the side. "You're both standing there as if you have no idea what comes next." She chuckled. "Go celebrate. Have fun. We'll see you here in the morning at eight A. M. sharp."

With a heart full of happiness and relief, Serenity could see her future brighten. As they exited the room, they both turned to the other.

"Where would you like to eat, Serenity?"

Serenity tilted her head to the side in thought and

shrugged. "Doesn't matter to me."

"There is a little diner down the street that makes an awesome fish dinner. It would be my pleasure."

"You're sure? "Serenity whispered, heart racing, and she rubbed her hands on her leotards as they walked out into the night air.

"I am certain." William gave her hand a reassuring squeeze as they strolled down the sidewalk away from the studio.

Up ahead, Serenity made Alice's form out as she headed

into the road without stopping. Serenity's eyes widened, and she took off with only one thought Let me make it, God.

Alice trudged, dragging her bag, and tears trailed down her face. She knew she had been jealous and allowed herself to be consumed by that hateful emotion. Swiping the tears away in frustration, April groaned. She had worked so hard, and it was all for nothing. And her exit ... Why did she storm out like an ungrateful child?

Alice kicked the wall of a building, breathing heavily.

Tears burned her eyes, and she lost the battle as they fell. She leaned her forehead against the cool bricks and pounded on the wall until her hand throbbed. She pushed herself away and continued into the murky night.

Alice hurried into the street without looking; she glanced up in horror at the blaring of a horn and saw headlights approaching her. Before she knew it, she was pushed hard and landed painfully on the pavement. She heard a thud, moved her hurting body around, and saw the still

Serenity on the ground and William rolling her over. As wailing sounds of sirens were heard in the distance.

References

Britannica, The Editors of Encyclopaedia. "ballet position". *Encyclopedia Britannica*, 30 Jun. 2023, https://www.britannica.com/art/ballet-position. Accessed 21 August 2023.

About the Author

Nicole Marie Woodcock lives in Pennsylvania. She has an Associate's Degree in psychology.

Nicole loves to read. She enjoys being creative. She loves to write and spends much time daydreaming. She cares for those around her and the environment.

She is the author of The Pendant Chronicles which includes two books.

The Frist is A Hidden Danger. The Second is Hidden Secrets.

Made in United States
Orlando, FL
25 February 2024